THIS BOOK BELONGS TO:

Hissss!

Mick Inkpen

Red Wagon Books
Harcourt, Inc.

San Diego   New York   London

T he sun was making
a shadow of Kipper
on the wall.

It was a hot day.

A very hot day.

K ipper lay on his blanket and sucked his drink through a curly-wurly straw.

"Today is a wading pool kind of day," he said.

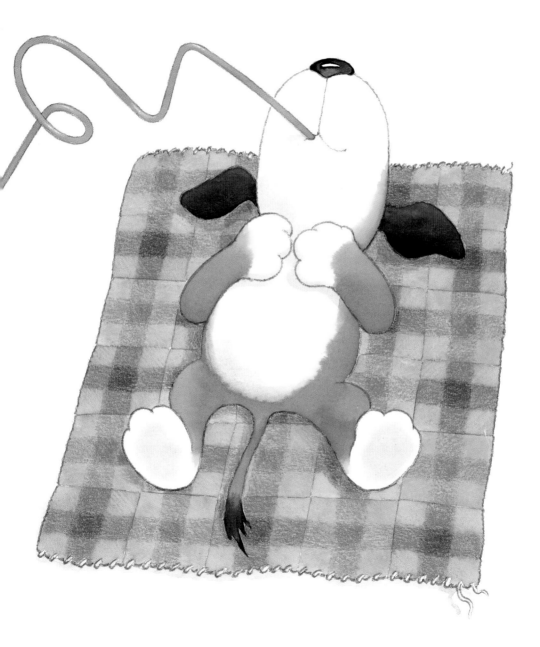

The wading pool was on the top shelf of the toy closet.

Kipper grabbed it and pulled enthusiastically.

The toys in the closet fell on Kipper's head.

Ouch!

It was hard work
blowing up the
wading pool.

So when Kipper was
finished, he turned on
the hose and went to
buy an ice-cream cone.

On the way back,
the ice cream
melted down Kipper's
paw and plopped into
a puddle.

"That's odd," said
Kipper. "It wasn't
raining when I left."

The puddle was as
big as a pond.
In the middle was
Kipper's wading pool,
looking very saggy.
"I know what has
happened," said Kipper.

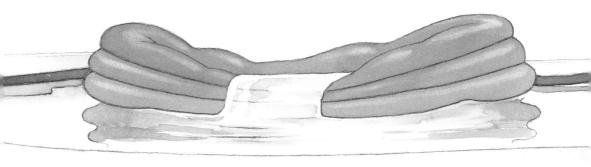

Kipper knelt down and listened very carefully to the wading pool.

With his big ears he could just hear a tiny,

tiny

hissss s s s s s s s s s s s s s s s s s s s s s s

ssssssssss!

Kipper took the
Band-Aid from
his head.
Ouch!

And he mended the
wading pool...

...which was clever,

wasn't it?

Library of Congress Cataloging-in-Publication Data
Inkpen, Mick.
Hissss!/by Mick Inkpen.
p. cm.
"Red Wagon Books."
Summary: On a hot summer day when Kipper the dog discovers
a leak in his wading pool, he fixes it in a very unusual way.
[1. Dogs—Fiction. 2. Summer—Fiction.] I. Title.
PZ7.I564Hi 2000
[E]—dc21 99-6728
ISBN 0-15-202415-8

A C E F D B

Printed in Hong Kong